The King's Chessboard

David Birch · pictures by Devis Grebu

PUFFIN BOOKS

DISCARD

For my mother, Doris Birch

D. B.

To Yvette, Sivan, Leo, and Alice

D. G.

PUFFIN BOOKS

Published by the Penguin Group

Penguin Putnam Books for Young Readers,

345 Hudson Street, New York, New York 10014, U.S.A.

Penguin Books Ltd, 27 Wrights Lane, London W8 5TZ, England

Penguin Books Australia Ltd, Ringwood, Victoria, Australia

Penguin Books Canada Ltd, 10 Alcorn Avenue, Toronto, Ontario, Canada M4V 3B2

Penguin Books (N.Z.) Ltd, 182-190 Wairau Road, Auckland 10, New Zealand

Penguin Books Ltd, Registered Offices: Harmondsworth, Middlesex, England

Originally published in hardcover by Dial Books for Young Readers
A Division of Penguin Books USA Inc.

Library of Congress Catalog Card Number: 87-20164

Manufactured in China by South China Printing Company Limited

First Puffin Pied Piper Printing 1993

ISBN 0-14-054880-7

A Pied Piper Book is a registered trademark of Dial Books for
Young Readers, a division of Penguin Books USA Inc.,

® TM 1,163,686 and ® TM 1,054,312.

30 29 28 27 26 25 24 23

THE KING'S CHESSBOARD

is also available in hardcover from

Dial Books for Young Readers.

Once, long ago, in what is now India, there lived a wise man who performed a service for the King of Deccan. In due course the King summoned the wise man to appear before him.

"You have served me well," said the King to the wise man. "What do you wish as a reward?"

The wise man bowed and said, "Serving Your Majesty is reward in itself."

"Indeed, indeed," said the King, "but it must not be said that the King does not reward those who serve him."

"Truly, sire," said the wise man, "I wish no other reward than to serve you again."

"But *I* wish you to be rewarded," said the King in a stern voice. There was a quiet murmuring among the councillors and nobles assembled in the great hall. The King was getting angry. But the wise man seemed not to notice.

"Truly, sire," the wise man said calmly, "I can think of no way you could reward me—"

"You *shall* choose a reward," said the King, "or I promise, you will wish you had!"

The wise man was silent for a long time. And then the small wooden chessboard next to the King seemed to catch his interest.

"Very well, sire," the wise man said at last. "I ask only this: Tomorrow, for the first square of your chessboard, give me one grain of rice; the next day, for the second square, two grains of rice; the next day after that, four grains of rice; then, the following day, eight grains for the next square of your chessboard. Thus for each square give me twice the number of grains of the square before it, and so on for every square of the chessboard."

Now the King wondered, as anyone would, just how many grains of rice this would be. He thought of grains of rice on a chessboard: one, two, four, eight, sixteen.... There were sixty-four squares. Would that be a pound of rice in all? The King wasn't sure.

At this point the Queen whispered to him, "It seems that the simplest thing to do would be to ask him how much rice that is."

Indeed, that would have been simple; but it would also have made it obvious to everyone that the King was not sure how much rice it was, and the King was too proud to let anyone think he was ever unsure of anything. So he did not ask the question. Instead, he smiled royally and said to the wise man, "Your complicated request is most simply granted."

This caused a stirring of laughter among the councillors and nobles, and as the wise man bowed and quietly left the hall, there was much amusement at this simple old man and his odd request.

To add to the humor the Grand Superintendent of the King's Granaries had a servant, wearing the most splendid garments, carry the first little grain of rice on a gleaming silver tray to the wise man's house. But the wise man merely thanked the servant and placed the grain on the first square of his chessboard.

When the King heard this, he placed a grain of rice on the first square of his own chessboard.

On the second day two grains of rice were sent to the wise man, and the King and the wise man each placed a grain of rice on the second square of his chessboard. And so it went: four grains of rice to the wise man on the third day and a grain of rice on the third square, and so on.

On the eighth day there was no servant in splendid dress, but only an ordinary granary worker bringing one hundred twenty-eight grains of rice in a small pouch. The wise man placed one grain on the eighth square of his chessboard and threw the rest to a bird outside his window. By now the King had quite forgotten the wise man and his rice, and it was left to a servant to place a grain on the eighth square of the King's chessboard.

The actual counting of the grains of rice was left to the Weigher of the King's Grain: two hundred fifty-six grains, then five hundred twelve, then one thousand twenty-four.

"Dear me," said the Weigher to himself on the twelfth day, "soon I'll be counting grains all day long." So instead of counting out two thousand forty-eight grains of rice, he simply weighed out an ounce of rice and sent it to the wise man.

Only four days later the wise man was sent a small bag of rice weighing sixteen ounces, or one pound. He placed one grain on the sixteenth square of his chessboard and gave the rest to a beggar.

But at the granaries the Weigher had become worried.

"Tomorrow," he said to himself, "it will be two one-pound bags, and the next day it will be four." He calculated the amounts: eight, sixteen, thirty-two.... When he got to two thousand forty-eight bags, he stopped in alarm. "I must tell the Grand Superintendent of the King's Granaries at once!"

But when he was actually standing before the Grand Superintendent, the Weigher became so nervous that he didn't say what he
meant to say.

"Your — Your Excellency," he stammered, "excuse me…the rice
sent to the wise man is…excuse me…How many small bags of rice are
there in the King's granaries?"

"What kind of question is that?" demanded the Grand Superintendent. "Weigher, have you been drinking?"

"N-no, Your Excellency," the Weigher said. Then he hurried back
to his scales and promised himself not to bother anybody again about
the wise man's rice.

It was only nine days later that the Grand Superintendent saw four granary workers carrying sacks of rice from the granary. Following them was a group of ragged children.

"Here! Stop!" shouted the Grand Superintendent. "Where are you going with the King's rice?"

When the children laughed at this, the Grand Superintendent demanded, "And why are these urchins so merry?"

"Your Excellency," said one of the granary workers, "we are carrying this rice to the wise man, who then gives it away to the poor and hungry."

"Impossible!" said the Grand Superintendent. "That fool of a Weigher has made some mistake."

But there had been no mistake.

It was explained how one grain became two and then four; grains became ounces; ounces became pounds; a bag became two bags; and today it was four sacks, each weighing one hundred twenty-eight pounds.

The Grand Superintendent said to himself, "Tomorrow there will be eight sacks—over half a ton! I must tell the King!"

But the King was away hunting in the mountains that day and the next. So on the day after that the Grand Superintendent had to send the wise man over a ton of rice. The next day it was two tons. And still the King had not returned to the palace. There was nothing to be done.... The next day four tons.... Then eight tons.

On the day after that, when the King returned, he heard a great cheering outside his palace. From his window he saw sixteen wagons, each carrying sixteen sacks of rice—over a ton on each wagon. The wagons were followed by a crowd of happy people.

"Where are those wagons going?" the King demanded.

"Sire," said the Grand Superintendent of the King's Granaries, "that is the rice being sent today to the wise man."

"Impossible!" said the King. "You have made some mistake!"

"I fear not, sire," said the Grand Superintendent, and began to explain how one grain became two, then one ounce became two ounces, then a pound became—

"Enough!" said the King. "Summon the royal mathematicians."

The mathematicians appeared and were ordered to determine how many tons of rice the King had in fact promised to the wise man. After an hour of calculating and recalculating, the Chief Mathematician rather nervously held up a slate with their answer for the total of all the rice that was to be sent for all of the sixty-four days.

As the King read the number he grew angrier and angrier. "Two hundred seventy-four billion, eight hundred seventy-seven million, nine hundred six thousand, nine hundred forty-four tons!

"Tons!" roared the King. "Tons! Deception and treason!" He then ordered everyone from his presence except the Queen.

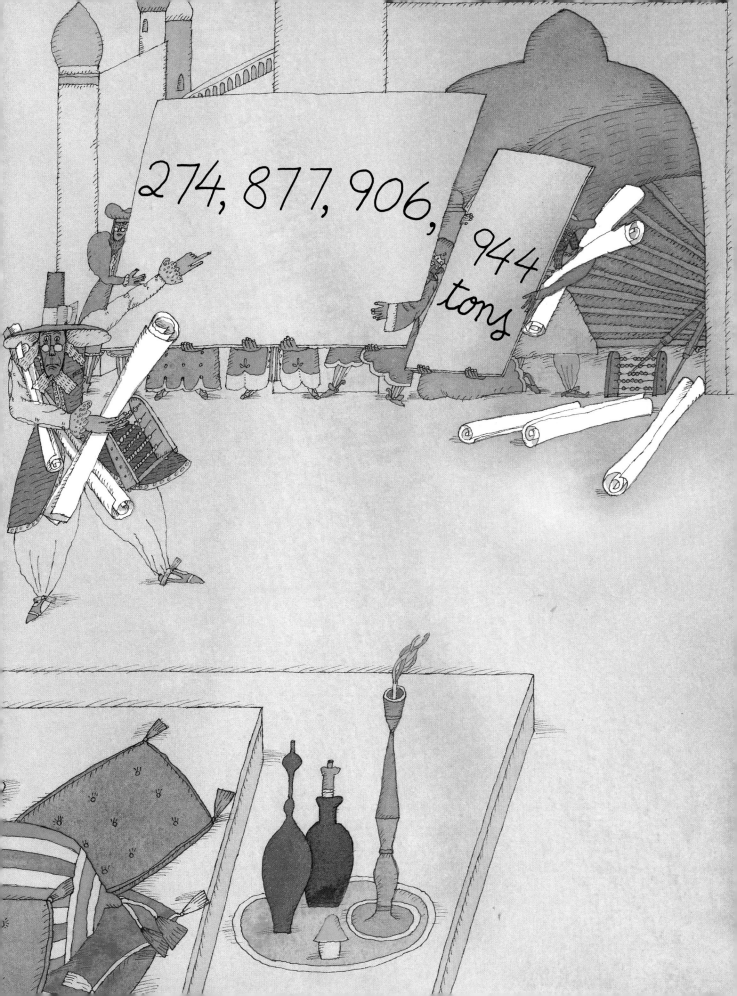

He sat and glared at his chessboard with its thirty-one grains of rice
—thirty-one days since he insisted the wise man should be rewarded.
After a time the Queen said to him, "You must ask the wise man to
release you from your promise. It is the only thing to be done."

But the King seemed not to hear.

Finally the Queen left him alone with his anger and silence. There he sat all that day and there he stayed all that night, dozing fitfully until he was awakened by the first light of morning.

Below he saw a line of thirty-two wagons leaving the granaries and huge, happy crowds following them.

The King sighed. He placed a grain of rice on the thirty-second square of his chessboard and then gave orders to summon the wise man to the palace.

"This must stop," said the King to the wise man. "There is not enough rice in all of India to reward you."

"No, indeed, sire," said the wise man. "There is not enough rice in all the world."

"Then," said the King, "since I have promised you the impossible, I command you as my loyal subject to tell me how you will be satisfied."

"But I *am* satisfied, sire," said the wise man. "It is as I tried to tell

you, sire. I have always been satisfied. It was *you* who insisted on rewarding me. It is *you* who must be satisfied."

As the wise man spoke these words all the splendid people in the great hall became very, very still.

"*Are* you satisfied, sire?" asked the wise man. And although he spoke quietly, everyone heard him as if he had shouted. No one whispered. No one moved.

"Yes," said the King at last. "Yes, I am satisfied."

Then he smiled at the wise man, not a happy smile perhaps, but a genuine smile. "And I understand," the King said, "that in all this you have done me yet another service."

"Then, sire, I am truly rewarded," said the wise man. With that he bowed very low and left the great hall.

The wise man returned to his simple home and quiet life. And although he was to serve the King many times afterward, the question of a reward never again arose.

The King ruled wisely and justly for many, many years, and to the end of his days he kept the chessboard with its thirty-two grains of rice to remind him of the wise man's lesson—how easy it is for pride to make a fool of anyone, even a king.